Johnson

SAMUEL TODD'S BOOK OF GREAT INVENTIONS

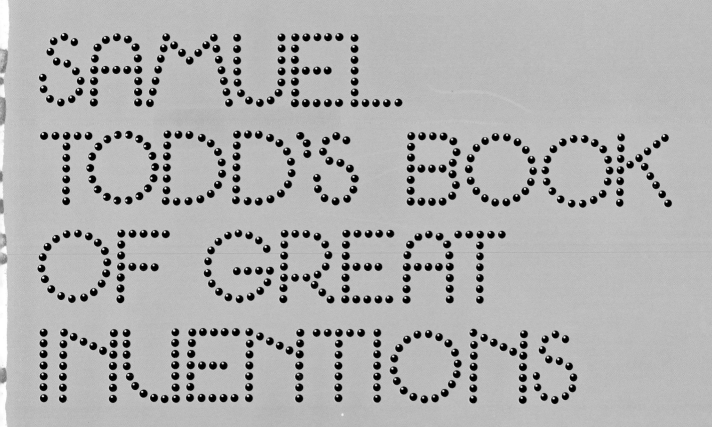

written and illustrated by

E. L. KONIGSBURG

A Jean Karl Book
ATHENEUM 1991 NEW YORK

Collier Macmillan Canada
TORONTO

Maxwell Macmillan International Publishing Group
NEW YORK OXFORD SINGAPORE SYDNEY

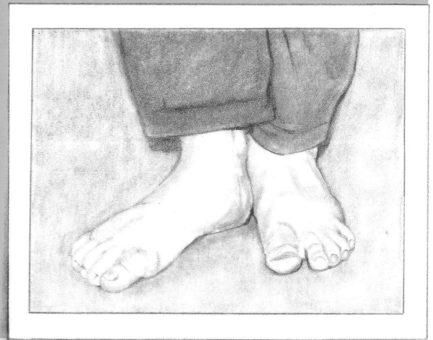

For Jean Karl
   —because silver anniversaries are rare in any relationship

Copyright © 1991 by E. L. Konigsburg

LIBRARY OF CONGRESS CATALOGING-IN-PUBLICATION DATA

Konigsburg, E. L.
   Samuel Todd's book of great inventions / written and illustrated
by E.L. Konigsburg.—1st ed.
      p.   cm.
   "A Jean Karl book."
   Summary: Samuel Todd shows readers some inventions that make his
day easier and better, including velcro, a thermos bottle, training
wheels, backpacks, and mittens.
   ISBN 0-689-31680-1
   1. Inventions—Juvenile literature.   [1. Inventions.]   I. Title.
T48.K59   1991
608—dc20   90-23688

Atheneum
Macmillan Publishing Company
866 Third Avenue
New York, NY 10022

Collier Macmillan Canada, Inc.
1200 Eglinton Avenue East
Suite 200
Don Mills, Ontario M3C 3N1

First edition
Printed in Hong Kong by South China Printing Company (1988) Ltd.
1   2   3   4   5   6   7   8   9   10

BOOKS BY E. L. KONIGSBURG

Jennifer, Hecate, Macbeth, William McKinley,
and Me, Elizabeth
From the Mixed-up Files of Mrs. Basil E. Frankweiler
About the B'Nai Bagels
(George)
Altogether, One at a Time
A Proud Taste for Scarlet and Miniver
The Dragon in the Ghetto Caper
The Second Mrs. Giaconda
Father's Arcane Daughter
Throwing Shadows
Journey to an 800 Number
Up from Jericho Tel
Samuel Todd's Book of Great Colors
Samuel Todd's Book of Great Inventions

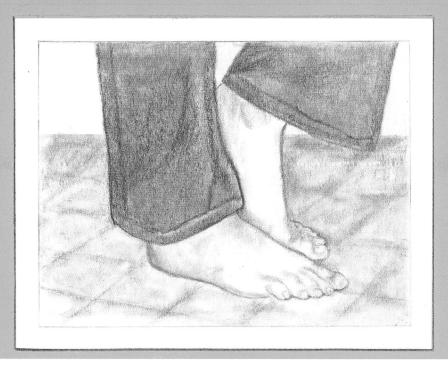

The second thing
I do every morning
is make sure that I am still
Samuel Todd.

Mirrors are a great invention.

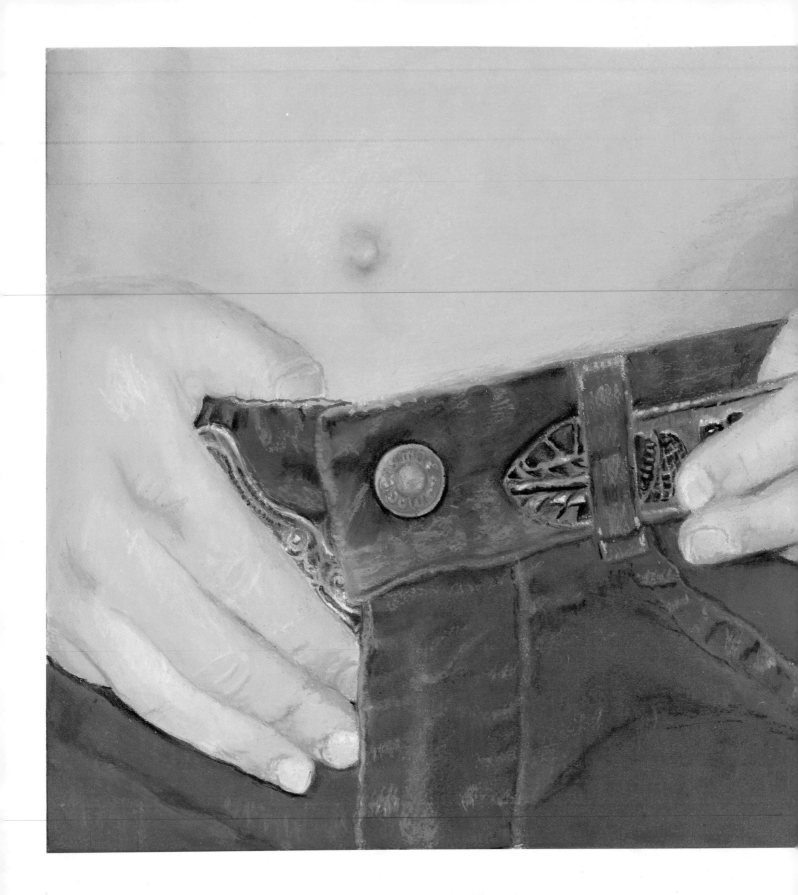

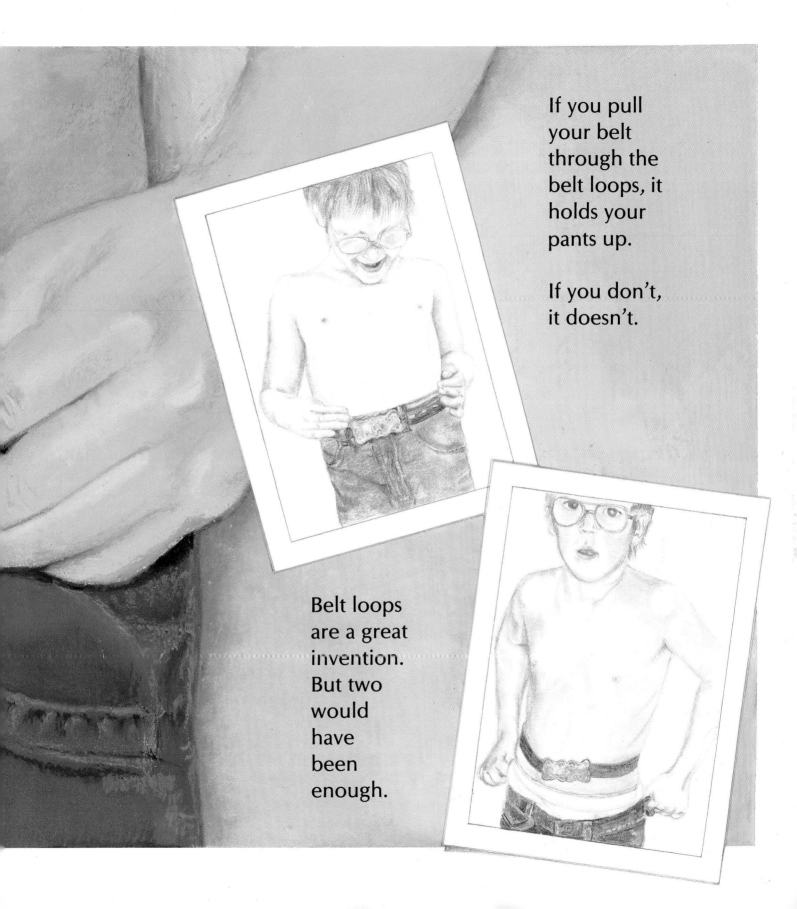

If you pull your belt through the belt loops, it holds your pants up.

If you don't, it doesn't.

Belt loops are a great invention. But two would have been enough.

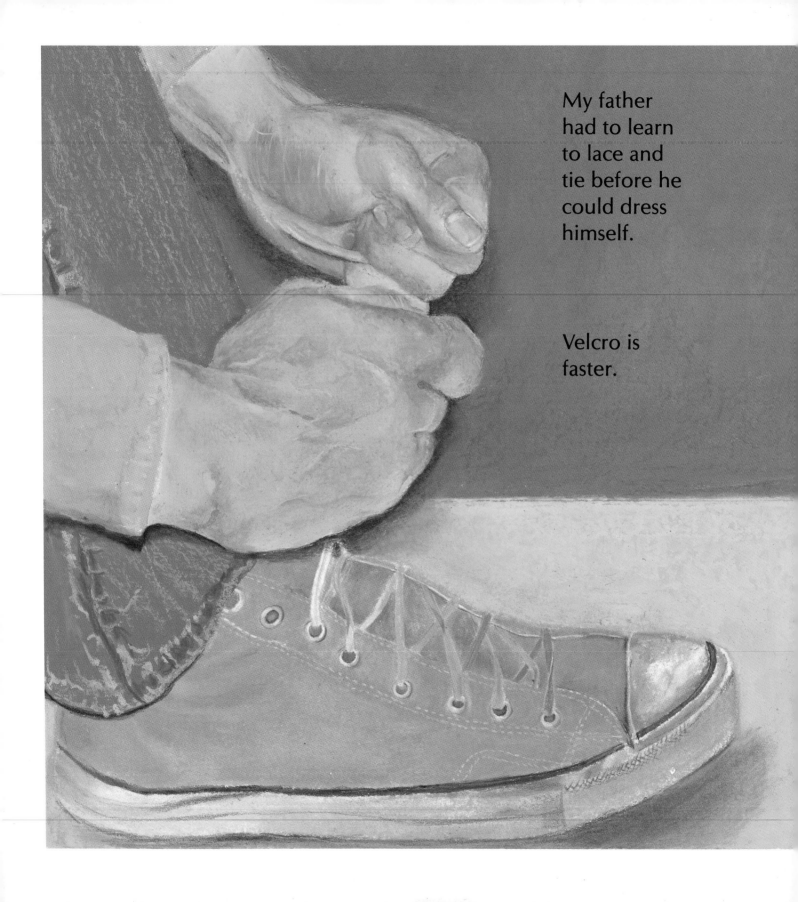

My father
had to learn
to lace and
tie before he
could dress
himself.

Velcro is
faster.

Velcro also beats buttons.

Mittens were invented to keep
hands warm, but someone
who wanted warm hands
and also wanted to zip
someone up or call someone
up or write something
down invented gloves.

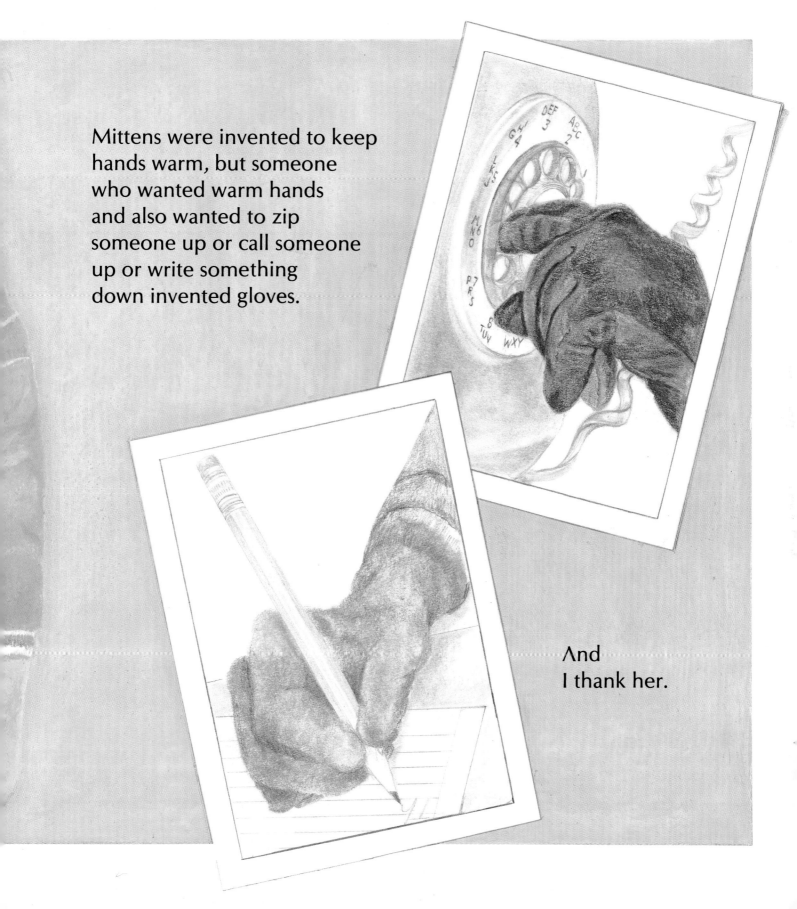

And
I thank her.

Without a backpack, the only thing you can do with your hands is hold the stuff that should be in your backpack.

What makes
a thermos bottle
a great invention
is that it keeps
hot soup hot
and
Kool-Aid cool
and
knows when
to do which.

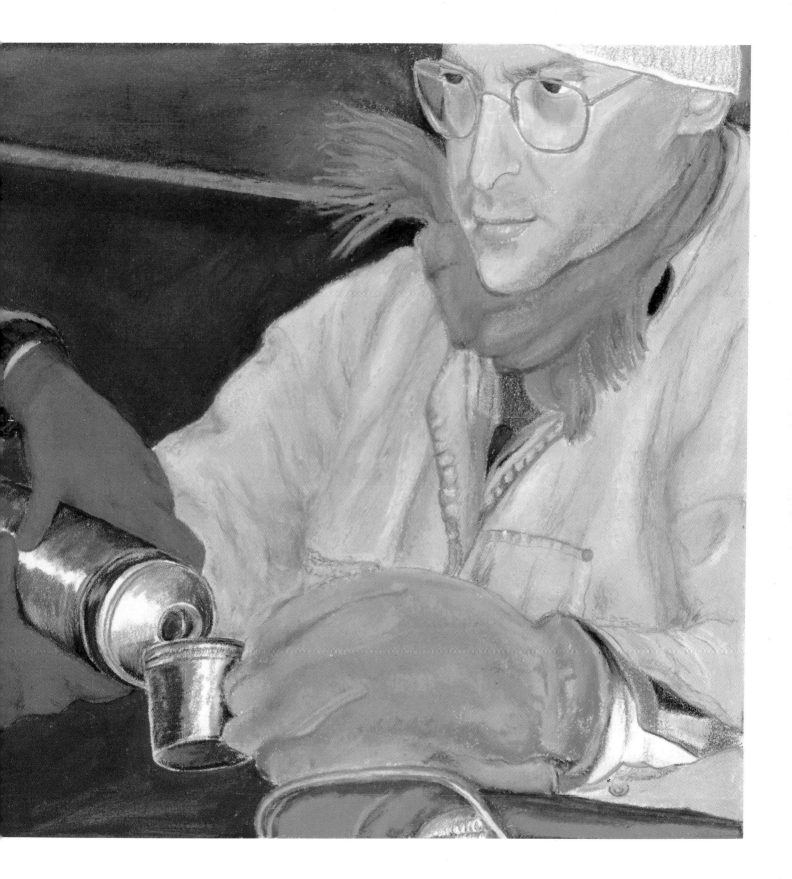

Training wheels are an invention
that makes four wheels twice
as good as three.

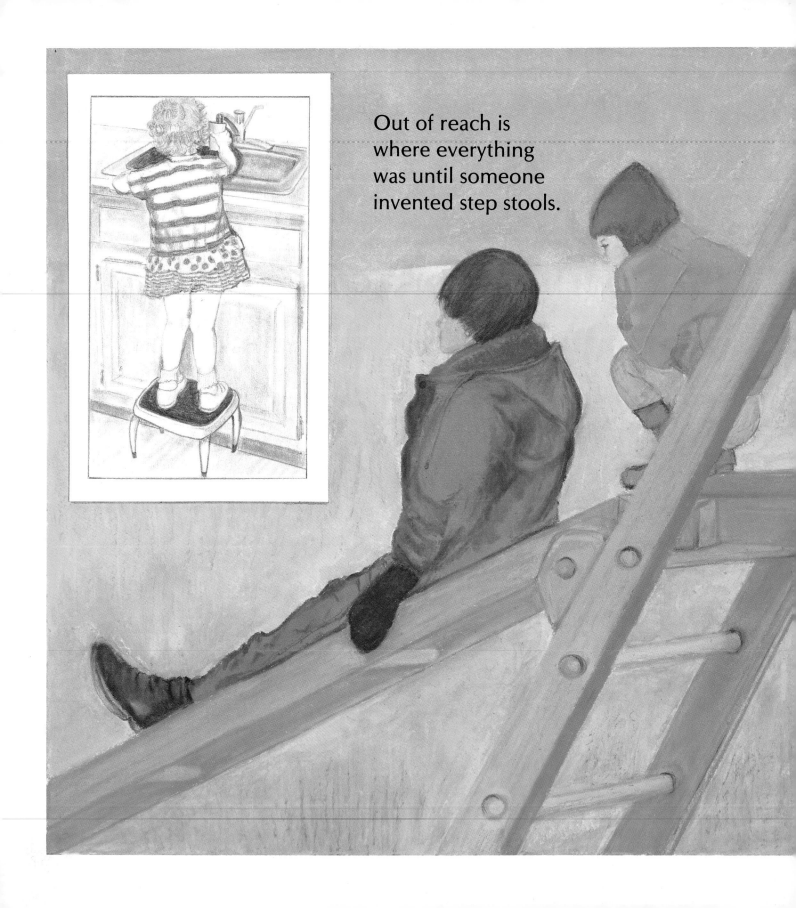

Out of reach is where everything was until someone invented step stools.

Ladders are the same thing, only taller.

Whoever
invented boxes
was a genius.
He invented
so many
different kinds.

Candles help you see when the lights go out,
and that's why they are a great invention.

They are also very useful on birthday cakes.

Halloween was
invented so
that no one
has to go
trick-or-treating
as his or her
same old self.

A little child invented the cuddle blanket.
You don't need it by the time you're ready to
lose your first tooth.
And my mother says that
when you're altogether grown up,
you won't think about it
even a couple of times
a week.

Rebecca and Martha call it a *ninny*.

Sarah calls it her *uh-oh*.

Anna calls it a *B*
and has four
of them.

Amy has a pillow.

Before I get into bed, I always look
to see if I'm still Samuel Todd.
Once I had chicken pox. Sometimes
I have chapped lips.

If my loose tooth comes out while
I sleep, tomorrow I'll be different.

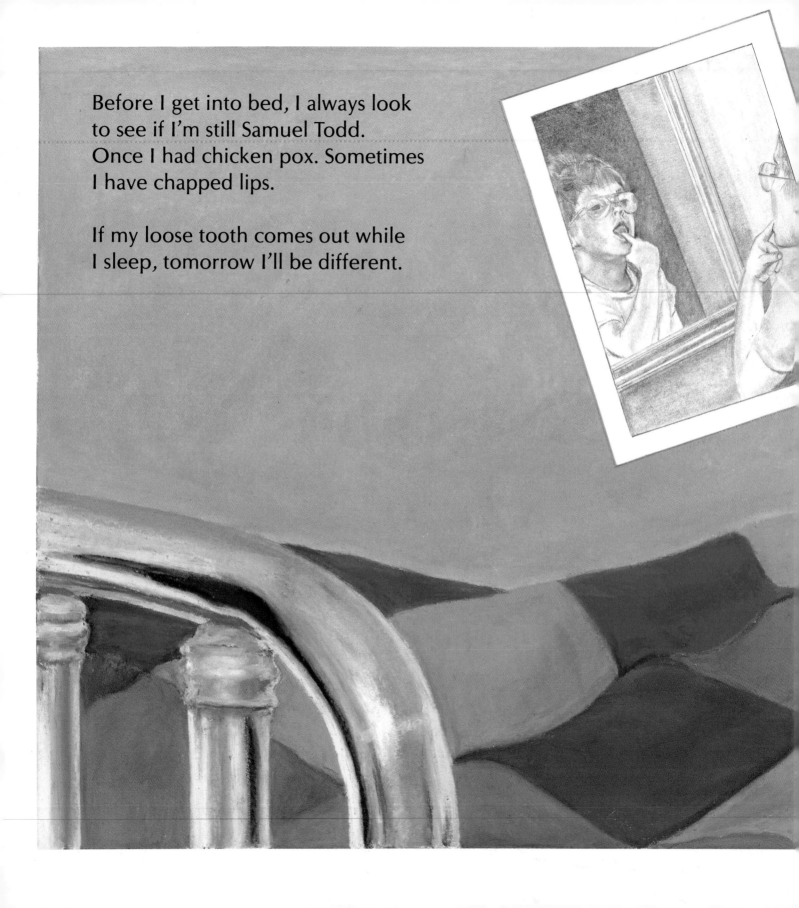

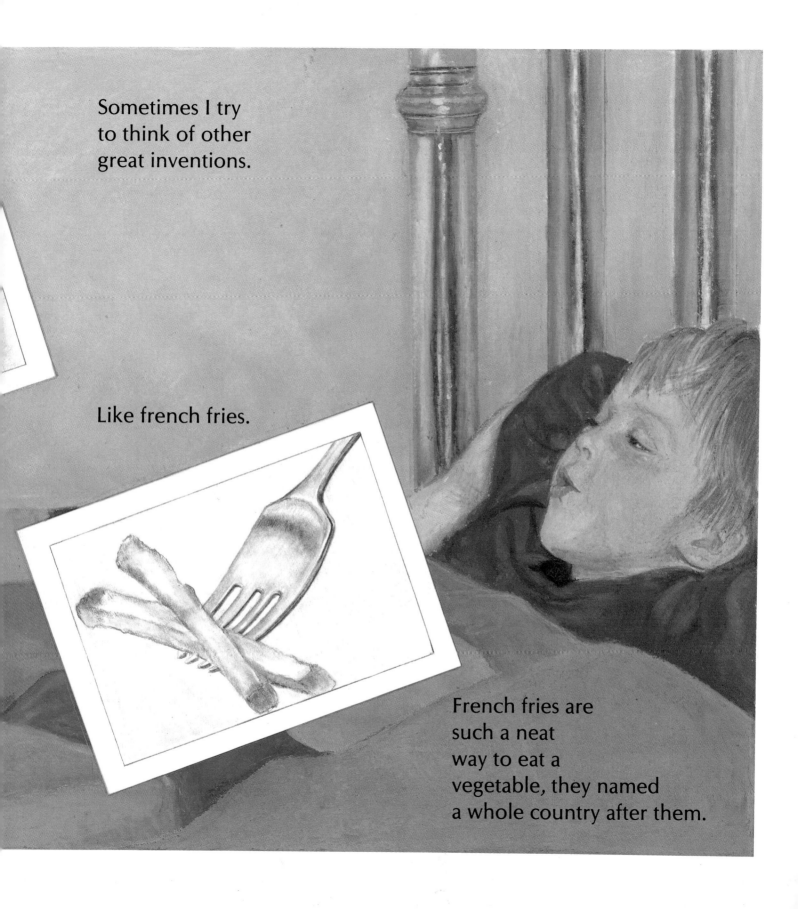

Sometimes I try
to think of other
great inventions.

Like french fries.

French fries are
such a neat
way to eat a
vegetable, they named
a whole country after them.

When I asked my mother and
father what they thought were
the great inventions, my mother
said the telephone, and
my father said television.

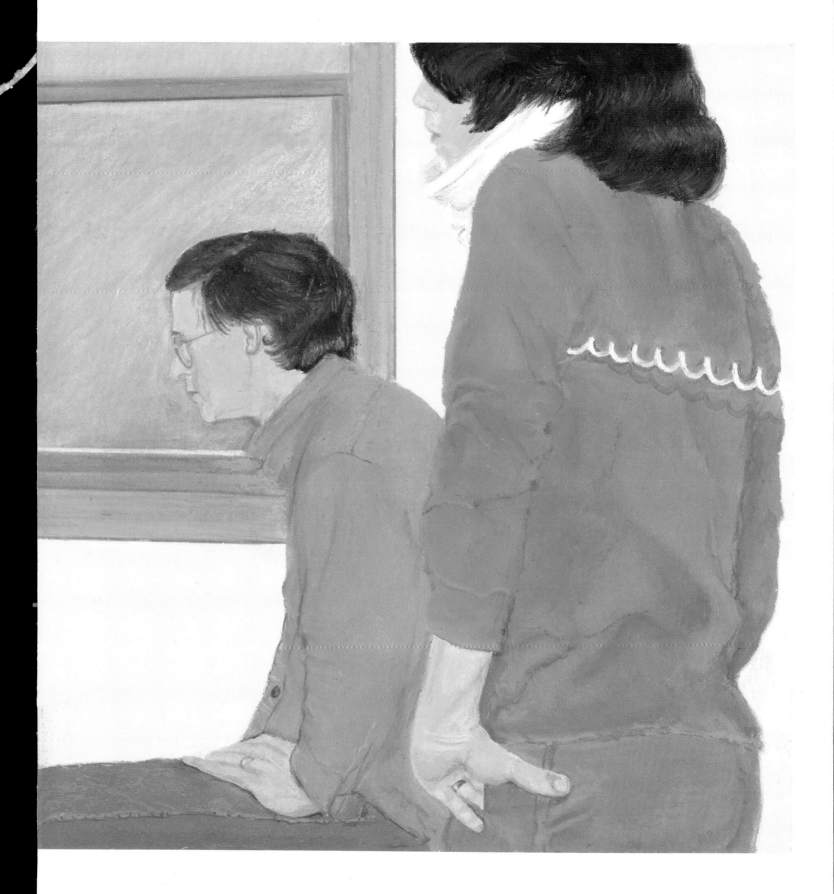

But I don't think the telephone
and television are great inventions.
They come with the house like
mothers and windows
and fathers and walls.